# The Case of the
# Double Trouble Detectives

# Read all the Jigsaw Jones Mysteries

A JIGSAW JONES MYSTERY®

# The Case of the
# Double Trouble Detectives

*by James Preller*
*illustrated by Jamie Smith*
*cover illustration by R. W. Alley*

A
**LITTLE APPLE**
PAPERBACK

SCHOLASTIC INC.
New York Toronto London Auckland Sydney
Mexico City New Delhi Hong Kong Buenos Aires

*Special thanks to*
*Howie Dewin*

ISBN 0-439-67804-8

Text copyright © 2005 by James Preller. Illustrations copyright © 2005 by Scholastic Inc. All rights reserved. Published by Scholastic Inc. SCHOLASTIC, LITTLE APPLE, A JIGSAW JONES MYSTERY, and associated logos are trademarks and/or registered trademarks of Scholastic Inc.

12 11 10 9 8 7 6                                              8 9 10/0

Printed in the U.S.A.                                              40
First printing, February 2005

# CONTENTS

# Chapter One

## Sister from Another Planet

My dad says that boys are from Mars and girls are from Venus.

He says he read it in a book. He says it was a national bestseller, sort of like Harry Potter for grown-ups. Go figure.

Anyway, I don't know about that. I always thought my mom was from Hackensack, New Jersey.

But when it comes to my teenage sister, Hillary, I guess anything is possible. Maybe she *is* from another planet. It would explain a lot.

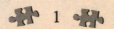

This is the conversation she had with my mom while we were all eating breakfast on Sunday morning. "I hate Mary Lou Betts," Hillary said.

"Don't say that word," my mother replied.

(Mom hates the word *hate* and gets mad whenever we use it.)

"Fine, then," Hillary snarled. "I really, really, really don't like Mary Lou Betts."

"Much better," my father groaned. "See how sweet you can be when you try?" Then he rubbed his eyeballs and poured a large mug of coffee.

"I thought Mary Lou was your best friend," I noted. "Why do you really, really, really not like her?"

Hillary rolled her eyes. "Because!" she snapped.

I wondered if maybe Hillary really was from Venus — and they kicked her off the planet. Teenagers, yeesh.

"Oh, Hill," my mother sighed as she set

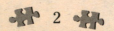

three stacks of pancakes in front of my brothers, Billy, Nick, and Daniel. "Mary Lou is practically part of the family. She's been your best friend since —"

"— since the third grade," Hillary interrupted. "But not anymore. Not after what she did on Friday."

This was getting interesting.

"What did she do?" I asked.

"She told Ricky Astacio that I thought he was cute," Hillary complained.

Billy made a clucking sound with his tongue. Nick giggled. Daniel asked for more syrup.

"Do you think he's cute?" my mother asked.

"He's gorgeous!" Hillary gushed, suddenly goo-goo-eyed. "But I don't want Ricky to know that. He'll think I have some kind of mad crush on him."

"But you DO have a crush on him," my mother said.

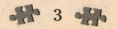 3

Hillary shook her head. "Just because I like him doesn't mean I *like*-like him," she explained.

"Hmm," my mom murmured doubtfully.

Hillary's cheeks flushed red. "The point is, Mary Lou had no right telling him." She rose from her chair with a clatter. "And I am never, *ever* going to speak with her again."

That's when I answered the telephone. After a moment, I turned to Hillary. "For you," I said. "It's Mary Lou."

Hillary scowled, lifted her nose in the air, and said, "Tell her I'm not home."

My parents frowned disapprovingly. I explained to Mary Lou that Hillary said she wasn't home. Mary Lou wasn't buying that, and who could blame her? "Hillary," I said, "Mary Lou wants to give you a message."

Hillary put her fingers in her ears.

And hummed, loudly.

I continued, "Mary Lou says that Ricky said that he thinks that you're cute, too."

Hillary's eyes nearly popped out of her head.

"Give me the phone, Jigsaw!"

Then Hillary grabbed the phone and ran into another room.

I looked around the kitchen table. "Weird," I concluded.

Grams looked at me and winked. "She's discovered boys."

"Run for the hills," Billy said with a laugh.

My dad peered over the newspaper. He wasn't laughing. "You're the detective, Jigsaw. If you can figure out that sister of yours, let me know. Because I haven't got a clue. Women are a mystery to me."

"They certainly are," my mother snapped.

My father looked at my mother. "What's wrong with you?" he asked.

"You don't remember, do you?" she said.

My dad shrugged and smiled. "I might

have remembered, unless I forgot," he joked.

"Men," my mom muttered.

Then she stormed out of the room in a huff.

Don't ask. Beats me.

But I was beginning to think that maybe my mom wasn't from Hackensack after all. Venus seemed more likely.

# Chapter Two
## Sporks and Skorts

Trouble is my business. I'm a detective. For a dollar a day, I make problems go away. I have a partner, Mila Yeh. She's my friend, too. Together we've found missing paintings and stolen falcons. We've tracked down ghosts and marshmallow monsters. When something goes wrong, we're the right detectives for the job.

We track down clues. We find suspects. We ask tough questions. And, hey, we stop for a tall glass of grape juice every once in

a while. A guy gets thirsty in this line of work.

I shouldn't brag, but like George Washington, I cannot tell a lie: We're the best detectives in the second grade. In fact, we used to be the ONLY detectives in the second grade. But these days, the mystery game has become pretty popular. Bobby Solofsky started his own detective business a while back. No biggie. Nobody ever hires him.

But today Mila came over with news. The bad kind.

We were down in my basement office. It's nothing special, just an old desk in a cluttered basement that I share with a washing machine and a bunch of rusty tools. On the wall behind my desk there's a sign that reads: JIGSAW JONES, PRIVATE EYE. The sign is just like me, nothing fancy. But it gets the job done.

Mila was pacing back and forth. She had

her Thinking Machine working overtime. She had just told me the news. Reginald Pinkerton Armitage III — the richest kid in town — had just started a new business.

You guessed it. A detective agency.

Mila slapped a flyer down on the desk. I read it:

**Reginald Pinkerton Armitage III**
# Secret Agent

* **Cool Gadgets!**
* **High-Tech Equipment!**
* **Top Secret!**

"I'm worried about this," Mila complained.

"Relax, Mila," I said. "Reginald can do what he wants. It's a free country."

"You don't get it, Jigsaw," Mila replied. "I'm worried about Reginald. He's just a

sweet kid. He doesn't know the first thing about being a secret agent."

I had to agree with her. Crime can be a rough business. And Reginald Pinkerton Armitage III was about as tough as a pair of silk pajamas.

"He'll get eaten alive," I said.

"Exactly," Mila said. "Unless we help him."

"I don't know, Mila," I replied. "Maybe Reginald doesn't want our help."

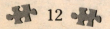

Mila started pacing again. She pulled on her long black hair. Mila said, "I heard Athena Lorenzo and Stringbean Noonan talking at the Music Studio this morning. Reginald has every detective supply that money can buy. He's got listening devices and microcameras. He's even got suction-cupped shoes that let him walk on the ceiling! Everybody thinks he's the greatest thing since . . . since . . ."

". . . since sporks?" I offered.

"Huh?"

"Sporks," I said. "You know, those plastic things you see every once in a while. Half forks, half spoons. Sporks. A great invention."

"Oh," Mila replied. "Like skorts?"

"Skorts?"

Mila nodded. "Half shorts, half skirt — a skort. All the girls wear them."

"I don't know anything about that," I said.

Mila rolled her eyes. "Forget sporks and skorts," Mila exclaimed. "Athena thinks Reginald is the hottest thing since . . . James Bond."

"Oh, please!" I laughed. "Reginald couldn't catch a cold if he ran around in a snowstorm wearing just his underwear. I doubt he's going to catch any bad guys."

"It's not something to laugh at," Mila shot back. "Reginald shouldn't be messing around with this stuff. He could get hurt."

Mila was right, I suppose. I poured myself a tall glass of grape juice. "Look," I said to Mila. "We've solved cases for everybody." I ticked some names off with my fingers. "Lucy Hiller, Geetha Nair, Bigs Maloney, Joey Pignattano . . . none of them are going to hire Reginald just because he's got a lot of expensive toys. How could he possibly get himself into any danger?"

Mila crossed her arms and frowned.

"Okay, fine," I relented. "If it will make you feel better, I'll go have a talk with Reginald Pinkerton Armitage."

# Chapter Three

### Reginald's House

About an hour later, I was set to visit Reginald Pinkerton Armitage III. That is, I put on a pair of clean socks.

A loud noise startled me — *SLAM!* — so I hustled into the living room. My father was standing by the front door, looking worried. Peering out the living room window, I could see my mother pulling the car out of the driveway. It looked like she was in a hurry to get somewhere.

"Is everything all right?" I asked my dad.

He blinked a few times. Scratched his

head. Then walked away without answering me.

I'd seen this kind of thing before. All parents fight sometimes. But it always gives me a sick feeling in my stomach. Sure, it was kind of gross when my parents kissed and snuggled. Nobody wants to see that. I don't like it in movies and I don't need to see it in real life. But when they argued, well, that was even worse.

All I knew was this: My dad was in

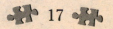

trouble. And it looked to me like he had no idea why.

Anyway, I had trouble of my own. So I set out on my bicycle to 86 Baker Street, the home of Reginald Pinkerton Armitage III. I'd been to his house before. It's about what you'd expect if you were visiting the king of a small country. But for an eight-year-old kid, the place was a bit much.

I knew that I'd see an enormous house and a front lawn the size of a football field. I knew I'd see white marble hallways and sparkling chandeliers. But I didn't expect to see a bunch of bicycles parked outside the house, next to skateboards and Rollerblades. I recognized most of the bikes. Some of my friends and classmates were already here. I wondered why.

I tucked in my shirt. Pulled down my hat. And did push-ups on the doorbell. It chimed: *Gong-gong-gong.*

Reginald's sister, Hildy, came to the door.

She seemed surprised to see me. "Oh, Jigsaw. I didn't know you'd be coming."

She invited me inside. I knew the house rules, so I kicked off my sneakers. I wiggled my toes. "See," I joked to Hildy, "this time there are no holes in my socks."

She smiled. "Very nice, Jigsaw. I see you're moving up in the world. But you better hurry. Madge just served refreshments," Hildy said. "Everyone is already here."

"Everyone?" I asked.

Hildy shrugged. "See for yourself." She gestured down the long hallway and told me to make two rights and a left at the antique grandfather clock. "They are in the backyard. Just open the door next to the indoor swimming pool."

"Great," I murmured. "If you hear a splash, then you'll know I made a wrong turn."

The backyard was huge. It looked like the playground of a large school. It had basketball hoops and trampolines, a climbing wall, and a jungle gym. To the left there was a large table covered by a white tablecloth. There was a crowd of kids gathered around silver trays of brownies, cookies, and other treats. I recognized a lot of my friends, laughing as they stuffed their faces with sugar-filled goodies.

Reginald Pinkerton Armitage III stepped forward. He was dressed in a black suit with a white shirt and a lavender tie. A hint of a handkerchief poked out from the right

breast pocket. His hair, as always, was perfectly slicked back. He looked like a pint-size version of James Bond. Which I guess was the idea.

He held out his hand in greeting. "Armitage," he purred. "Reginald Pinkerton Armitage the Third. At your service."

"Gee, Reg," I said. "I didn't realize you were having a party."

Reginald pressed the tips of his fingers together. "It's my Grand Opening," he

explained. "I daresay that it's good of you to make it, Jones. I feared you might be jealous."

"Nah," I said with a smile. "I'm happy for you. But tell me, why are you talking so fancy?" I asked. "It sounds like you swallowed a canary."

"Indeed," Reginald replied. He tilted his head and gazed at me strangely. With great effort, he raised one eyebrow. I could tell that he was trying hard to look dapper and stylish. "Perhaps you don't realize," he purred. "I'm a secret agent now."

"Some secret," I replied. "The news is all over town. To tell you the truth, Reg, that's why I'm here."

"Oh, really?"

"Yeah — oh, really," I echoed. "I think you're making a big mistake."

Reginald frowned. "Come to my office," he said. "We can talk in private."

# Chapter Four

## The Tough Guy

I followed Reginald inside the house. We walked down another long hallway and through a gaggle of doors. As we walked, I thought back to the first time I met Reginald.

He had called me to his house. He had a job for Mila and me. That was fine with us. That's when we solved the mystery of the golden key.

Reginald sure paid me back for that favor. Not too long after that, I lost a valuable watch. I was in a real jam. Thanks

to Reginald's last-second help, I was saved in the nick of time. So I figured I owed Reginald Pinkerton Armitage III.

Jigsaw Jones never forgets a favor.

Sure, some of the other kids may have thought of Reginald as "the rich kid." A fancy kid who doesn't go to regular schools and who rides around in helicopters for kicks. But I thought of him as "the nice kid." Mila called him "the lonely kid" who tries too hard.

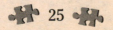

We became friends. What can I say? I like the guy, even if he does eat cucumber sandwiches.

I ended my stroll down memory lane when Reginald proudly announced, "My new office."

"I'll say," I clucked. The room was clean and large. It had leather armchairs, an oak desk covered with phones and other gadgets, and thick carpeting that made me feel like I was walking on fluffy clouds. Four large television screens filled the wall behind the desk. "It's okay," I admitted.

Reginald held up a finger. "One moment, Jones." Reginald glanced at his wrist, flipped open a weird thingy on his watch, and spoke into it. "Gus, I'll be leaving within the hour. Please have the limo ready."

"What kind of watch is that?" I asked.

Reginald sniffed. "It's a communicator, actually," he explained. "The latest thing.

Father picked it up while on a business trip to the Far East. It's also a stopwatch, thermometer, calculator, and compass."

"Swell," I groaned. "Does it make French toast, too?"

Reginald clapped his hands with glee. "Ha! You are the funny one, Jones! Actually, every secret agent needs one. I'm surprised you don't own one yourself."

I frowned. "There are lots of things I don't own, Reginald."

Reginald sat behind his desk. He leaned back in his chair, hands folded behind his head.

I cleared my throat. "Well, I'll be honest with you, Reginald. I don't think you're cut out for the secret agent business."

Reginald stared unhappily at his polished fingernails.

"No offense," I quickly said. "It's just that this line of work can get pretty rough sometimes."

"I can be rough," Reginald said. He politely silenced a burp with the back of his hand.

"Sure, you're as rough as a pussycat," I said. "Why in the world would a guy like you want to get mixed up in this racket?"

# Chapter Five

## A Knock at the Door

Reginald smiled. He gestured to the bank of television screens. "Look around, Jones. It's all the latest technology. I have everything I need. Microcameras and underwater walkie-talkies, laptop computers and motorized scooters. You name the gadget, I've got it." He paused, then stated, "I'm in it for the adventure! The thrills, spills, and chills!"

The poor kid had seen too many movies. I eyeballed him carefully. "How many cases have you solved, exactly?"

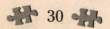

Reginald's eyes widened. "Cases? Actual cases?"

"Yeah, the actual kind," I replied.

"Why, none, yet," Reginald admitted sheepishly. "But I'm just getting started."

"None," I repeated. "You'll learn there is more to being a secret agent than owning a bunch of fancy gizmos. It takes old-fashioned detective work, the kind where you roll up your sleeves and get a little messy."

"Oh, really, Jones?" Reginald scoffed. "What makes you so smart?" I could see that he was getting upset.

I sighed and stood to leave. "I'm not so smart, but I have been around the block a few times," I answered. "Maybe I do know some things. For example, you just ate a hot dog before I arrived. Maybe you were in a hurry. I figure you drank a couple of glasses of cherry soda. You should be careful about that. It rots your teeth. Then you polished it all off with a brownie."

Reginald blinked in surprise.

"How am I doing so far?" I asked.

"I . . . um," Reginald stammered. "Er . . . How did you know?"

I smiled. "I'm a detective, Reginald. It's my business. I see things." I pointed to his chest. "There's a fresh mustard stain on your tie. You've burped twice in the last five minutes. I can smell the cherry soda on your breath. Plus, there are crumbs on

your jacket." I reached over, plucked one off, and popped it into my mouth. "Madge makes delicious brownies."

Suddenly, there was a sharp knock on the door.

Athena Lorenzo burst into the room.

"Reginald, thank goodness!" she exclaimed. "I've been looking all over for you! I'm in big trouble!" Athena reached out and grabbed his hand. "My mother's pearl earrings. They've been STOLEN!"

I instantly reached for my detective journal and flipped to a clean page. "Easy, Athena," I interrupted. "Tell us what happened."

Still holding Reginald's hand, Athena turned to look at me. From the expression on her face, she could have been staring at an eight-hundred-pound gorilla wearing silver ballet slippers.

"I came here to hire Reginald," she said.

"Sure," I said. I snapped my journal closed. "I was just trying to help."

Reginald walked briskly to the door and opened it. "I shall not need your help," he said. "I can handle this myself." With a sharp tilt of his head, Reginald told me to hit the road.

I began to protest. "But . . ."

I stopped to look at Reginald. His back was straight. His chin was high. He was proud.

"But . . . what?" Reginald asked sharply.

I swallowed hard and turned to Athena. "But . . . Reggie is going to do a great job, Athena. You picked the right man."

There was nothing left to do. I pulled my hat down tight and quickly said my so-longs. They thought I was leaving, but I had other ideas. I shut the door. I soundlessly slid to the floor, my ear pressed to the door.

Reginald Pinkerton Armitage III was going to get my help whether he wanted it or not. Like I said before, I never forget a favor.

# Chapter Six

## Right? Write!

I handed Mila a note on the school bus Monday morning. It looked like this:

REGINA LDHA SHI SFIR STCA SEI TIST HE
MY STE RYOFTH ESTOLENP EAR LEARRI NGS

Mila mused about it for a few moments. "A space code," she murmured.

She took out a pencil and slowly drew lines between certain letters. Like this:

"The spaces are in the wrong places," Mila noted. "Now I can read it: *Reginald has his first case. It is the mystery of the stolen pearl earrings.*"

I told Mila what I knew.

"You listened through the door?" Mila said approvingly. "Wow, sneaky."

"I only heard a little bit," I said. "There were footsteps coming and I had to get out of there."

According to Athena, she had a sleepover party on Saturday night with Geetha Nair, Lucy Hiller, and Helen Zuckerman. At some point the next day, Athena discovered that the pearl earrings were missing.

"Does she suspect anyone?" Mila asked.

I raised both my hands, palms up. "No idea," I said. "Reginald didn't ask the right

questions. He was more interested in showing Athena that nutty watch of his."

"I'll snoop around," Mila said. We agreed to meet at recess by the tire swing.

When we got to room 201, there was a lot of chatter about the hot new secret agent in town. Everybody gushed about suction-cupped shoes and bow-tie cameras. Yeesh.

*Clap-clap.* Ms. Gleason, our teacher, clapped her hands.

*Clap-clap,* we replied. It was time for schoolwork.

Ms. Gleason wrote pairs of words on the board.

EYE    WEEK    NO      NEW     ONE
I      WEAK    KNOW    KNEW    WON

"What do you notice about these word pairs?" Ms. Gleason asked.

Danika Starling had the answer. "They sound the same, but they mean different things."

Ms. Gleason smiled. "Exactly, Danika. I just thought of a new one. She wrote on the board.

PAIRS
PEARS

Does anyone know what we call these word pairs?" she asked.

"Fruit?" Joey Pignattano offered hopefully.

Ms. Gleason pointed to the board. "That would be *pears,* Joey, not *pairs.*"

Poor Joey. He was always thinking about food.

Ms. Gleason explained that they were called homophones: words that sound the same but are spelled differently and mean different things.

"Homophones are a lot of fun," Ms. Gleason told us. "Many jokes and riddles

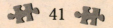

are based on homophones. For example, what's black and white but red all over?"

"A newspaper!" called out Bigs Maloney.

"A skunk with a nosebleed!" Helen shouted.

Ms. Gleason laughed. "I'm glad you're enjoying this," she said. "That joke is based on the homophones 'read' and 'red.'"

We spent more time messing around with homophones, filling in sentences, even making up our own riddles.

"For homework this week," Ms. Gleason said, "I'm going to issue a homophone challenge."

"A what?" I asked.

"It's like a mystery, Jigsaw," Ms. Gleason explained. "I want you all to try to find homophones as you go through the day. Together, we'll make a classroom list."

"I think I just thought of a joke," Geetha Nair said.

"Oh, let's hear it," Ms. Gleason replied.

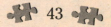

Quiet Geetha, who hardly ever spoke, said in a whisper: "What did one bunny say to the other bunny?"

The class was stumped.

So Geetha softly answered her own riddle, "I'm having a bad *hare* day!"

Soon everybody was making up bad jokes.

Then it was time for lunch. I was hungry. So I *eight* a lot!

# Chapter Seven

## Up a Tree

At recess Mila and I met at the tire swing and decided to stake out Athena's house after school. (Note to self: STAKE and STEAK — more homophones!) After all, a good detective, or even a bad secret agent, would have to visit the scene of the crime.

So we headed to Athena's house as soon as school let out. Then we ducked behind a row of hedges and waited. We figured that Reginald would be along at any moment.

Mila suddenly put her fingers to her lips. "Shhh. Did you hear that?" she whispered.

I listened. I heard the rustling of tree branches. And moaning. And groaning. And, yes, even whimpering. I pointed to an apple tree at the side of Athena's house. "There's somebody up there," I said.

We walked to the base of the tree. High up in the branches, we saw a familiar face.

"Reginald?" Mila called up.

"Oh . . . er . . . yes, I think so," he chirped.

"What are you doing up there?" Mila asked.

"Well, er, I was up here with my telescopic lens and . . . um . . . I'm sort of stuck. More or less," Reginald admitted.

"You are stuck in a tree," I noted.

"Well, yes," Reginald bleated.

"Why?" I had to ask.

"It seemed like something a secret agent would do," Reginald called down.

"Would you like some help?" I offered.

Reginald said that he'd like that very much.

Getting a boost from Mila, I scampered up the tree. Reginald's right foot was badly wedged between two branches. I pushed and pulled and twisted it until he was free. "Follow me down," I told him. "Be careful. This is an old tree."

"It's a little scary up here," Reginald said. There was fear in his voice.

"Nice and easy," Mila said. "One step at a time. But whatever you do, don't grab that branch to your left. It looks dead."

"This branch?" the secret agent asked.

*CRACK.*

*Oooofff.* Whoops. Ouch. Oh, dear. *Scratch, BOOM.*

Down he tumbled, his fall cushioned by a thicket of bushes.

"Reginald! Are you okay?!"

Slowly, painfully, Reginald stood up. His clothes were torn. His glasses were bent. And his hair was a disaster.

"You don't look so hot," I observed.

# Chapter Eight
## Teamwork

A few minutes later, we had Reginald brushed off and cleaned up. Okay, he still looked like a mess — and he was limping — but I figured he'd live.

"Now can we help you on the case?" I asked.

Reginald felt the side of his face. It was already turning black-and-blue. "Yes," he said. "That would be kind."

"Good," Mila said happily. "What have you learned so far?"

Reginald frowned. "How not to climb trees?" he moaned.

"Let's talk to Athena," I suggested.

Reginald wearily lifted a giant gym bag. It looked like it weighed a ton.

"What's in there?" Mila asked.

"Just, you know, important secret agent stuff," Reginald said. "Cameras, fingerprint kits, night-vision goggles, disguises, my bunny slippers, a tuning fork, a Swiss army knife, and —"

"Forget that junk," I said. "Let's try this my way."

We knocked on Athena's door. She brought us into her bedroom (Ack! What a mess!) and soon we had a list of suspects.

I wrote in my journal:

## SUSPECTS
Geetha Nair
Lucy Hiller
Helen Zuckerman

Mila frowned. "Aren't these your best friends?" she asked Athena.

Athena nodded. "Yeah, that's what stinks about this."

"I agree," Mila said. "I don't figure any of these girls for a thief."

I read from my notes. "Okay, Athena. You said that during the sleepover, you were playing dress-up."

Athena looked at Reginald. She blushed. "Actually, we call it 'Pretty Pretty Princess.'"

Yeesh.

"You had all the jewelry laid out on your dresser right here?" I asked.

Athena nodded. "I wasn't supposed to be using my mother's jewelry," she admitted. "At one point, she knocked on the door and startled us. So I swooped everything into my sock drawer."

She opened the drawer to show us. I started to poke around in it, but Athena quickly said, "They're not in there. I looked a hundred times. I found everything except for the pearl earrings."

Reginald coughed. "Um, Jones. This is all very educational. But shouldn't we be messing around with decoder rings or something cool like that?"

I ignored him.

"How about dusting the area for fingerprints?" he suggested.

I shook my head.

"Running a computer analysis of the tap water?" he asked hopefully.

"Those are wonderful ideas," I said, "if we were the Spy Kids and this was a Hollywood movie. But this is real life. Let's just try to use some brainpower."

Reginald sat on the edge of the bed, disappointed.

"After your mother left," Mila said to Athena, "did you play 'Pretty Pretty Princess' again?"

Athena shook her head. "No, we watched a DVD and went to sleep."

"So no one touched this sock drawer after your mother knocked on the door?" I confirmed.

Athena thought for a moment. Slowly, her face brightened. "Geetha's feet were cold. I let her borrow a pair of baggy old sweat socks."

"Hmmmmm," Mila mused. "The pearl

earrings, were they posts or the clip-on kind?"

Athena smirked. "They were posts, of course, not cheap clip-ons. They are my mother's pearl earrings. My dad gave them to her for their anniversary. She loves them. That's why I'm sooo dead if I can't find those earrings."

"Are you thinking what I'm thinking?" I asked Reginald.

He looked at me blankly. "Care to give me a hint, Jones?"

"You've got to find those socks," I said.

# Chapter Nine

## What's Eating Mom?

When I got home, everything seemed normal. Daniel and Nick were doing their homework at the dining room table. Hillary had locked herself in the hall closet with the telephone. "She's talking with Mary Lou about that boy," Nick explained.

I sat down next to my dog, Rags, and scratched his ears. In thanks, Rags licked my hand. I could have lived without the good manners. Yuck.

My mother seemed like her usual happy self.

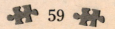

Until my dad came home. Then suddenly, the house got very cold. My mom grumbled and banged around from room to room, cleaning furiously. That was a bad sign. When she was angry, she cleaned.

I went to find my oldest brother, Billy. He was lying in his room, reading.

"What's going on with Mom and Dad?" I asked him.

Billy set aside the book. He propped

himself up on his elbows. "She's giving him the silent treatment."

"Why?" I wondered.

Billy shrugged. "Nobody knows."

"So, um, how does the silent treatment work, exactly?" I asked.

"Easy, you just stop talking to the person," Billy answered.

I scratched the back of my neck. Maybe I looked a little worried. Because Billy said, "Don't fret, Jigsaw. It will be okay. They once did this for four whole days."

"Really?"

Billy smiled. "Yep. You don't remember, because you're such a pip-squeak." Then he reached over and put me in a headlock.

It was my job to take out the garbage after dinner. For some reason, my father followed me to the curb. He asked, "So, how's the detective business these days?"

"It's going okay," I answered.

My father ran his hand through his hair. He looked toward the house. "Um, how'd you like to do me a favor, son?" he asked.

"Sure, Dad," I said. Inside my head I was thinking that I'd just discovered new homophones to add to my list: SON and SUN.

"It's about your mom," he said in a whisper. "She's mad at me for something. But I have no idea what."

"Oh," I said. "You need a detective to solve the mystery for you."

My dad nodded his head. "Well, yeah, I guess I do."

"I get a dollar a day," I said. "In advance."

"You want to charge me?" my father said in surprise.

I stretched out my hand, palm up. "That's the way the world works, Dad," I told him. "Besides, jigsaw puzzles don't grow on trees, you know."

My dad muttered something about "highway robbery" and "kids these days," but he eventually forked over the cash.

Then my dad slapped his head. "Whoops, I nearly forgot. There's a big game on TV!"

He raced into the house. Typical Dad. He was always forgetting something.

# Chapter Ten

## *Girl Talk*

I dug out my detective journal when I got inside the house.

I turned to a clean page and wrote:

What's eating Mom?

I thought about the things that usually made her upset. Had Dad left his muddy shoes on the living room rug? Did he leave the milk out? Or maybe, like me, he left the toilet seat up?

No, none of those things seemed right.

This was something that made her more upset than that stuff. We made messes every day. That was just regular living. Whatever Dad did, it had to be something really, really bad.

I decided to talk to Hillary. After all, she was a girl.

Mary Lou had just come over. They were supposed to be studying for a test. Instead, they were in Hillary's room doing weird stuff with their hair and giggling a lot. "Can I come in?" I asked.

"Just for a minute," Hillary said. "We're having a girl talk."

"Well, I don't want any part of that," I said. "But I do need your advice."

We talked about Mom and Dad. And about the silent treatment. "Why would someone do that?" I asked.

Hillary and Mary Lou exchanged glances. Then they both rolled around on the bed,

laughing. It was true. Teenage girls really were from Venus.

"Come on," I insisted. "This is important. Do you think Dad did something bad?"

Hillary made a face. "Get real, Jigsaw. Daddy worships Mom. He'd never do anything wrong on purpose."

Mary Lou tapped a finger on her lips thoughtfully. "Maybe it's not something he did," she said.

"What do you mean?" I asked.

"Maybe it's something he *didn't* do," she said.

"Like not doing the dishes or something like that?" I wondered.

"No, it would have to be a lot worse," Hillary said. "You don't use the silent treatment unless you are really, really mad. It's like the ultimate weapon."

Mary Lou nodded. "The cold shoulder. It's the best way to hurt a friend," she said.

"Revenge is like ice cream," Hillary said.
"It's a dish best served cold."

I had no idea what she was talking about.

It was getting close to bedtime, and now
I was more confused than ever. But I did
know one thing.

I was suddenly very, very hungry for ice
cream.

Maybe there was chocolate chip cookie
dough in the freezer.

# Chapter Eleven

## Case Closed

Reginald Pinkerton Armitage III visited on Tuesday night. A long black car dropped him off by the sidewalk.

"Jones, Mila," Reginald said when we opened the door. "I'm glad you're home."

"Come on in," I said. "What's up?"

We led Reginald into my office in the basement. Boy, it sure looked like a dump compared to his place. Oh, well. Money's not everything. Like Popeye says, "I yam what I yam."

"We heard that you solved the case," Mila said.

Reginald shrugged. "Yes, the earrings got caught in the thick socks — just as you suspected," he said. "Geetha had no idea they were stuck there. Luckily, I got to Geetha's house just before the socks went into the wash."

"Nice job, Reginald!" Mila congratulated him.

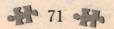

He looked down at the floor. Then into my eyes. "You guys solved the mystery, not me," he said. "I know that." With his right pinkie, Reginald pushed his glasses from the tip of his nose closer to his face. "You were right all along. I'm not cut out to be a secret agent man."

I exchanged glances with Mila. "But what about the thrills, spills, and chills?" I asked.

Reginald grimaced. "I would prefer to avoid any more spills, thank you very much."

We all laughed at that.

"Besides," he added, "secret agent work isn't what I thought it would be. Most of the time it's just talking and listening and looking at things. Kind of dull, if you ask me."

I smiled.

"What about all your electronic gizmos and gadgets?" I asked.

"You can borrow that stuff anytime you want," Reginald said. He shook my hand

and gave Mila a hug. "Thanks for looking out for me, guys. You're good friends."

It was nice to hear. (Hey, more words for my homophone list: HEAR and HERE!)

"Right now, I need a warm bath," Reginald said with a contented sigh. He flicked up his fancy wristwatch. "Excuse me, I must give my limo driver, Gus, a ring."

While Reginald talked into this strange little phone, Mila gave me a wink.

Suddenly, it hit me. "What did you say, Reginald?"

He looked at me blankly. "I have to call my driver, Gus."

"No." I shook my head. "You said that you had to give him a ring."

Reginald scratched his nose. "Yes. So?"

"The word ring is almost a homophone," I said. "Give him a ring. That means to call somebody. The way a bell rings. Or the other kind of ring," I said. "Like a wedding ring."

I gave Reginald a pat on the back. "Thanks, pal. I think you just helped me solve a case!"

Reginald stood there, looking surprised. Finally, a grin swept across his face. "I guess we're even!"

# Chapter Twelve

## *Ring! Ring!*

Mila and I found my father in the den. He was watching television by his lonesome, looking weary.

"I think I know why Mom is mad," I told him.

He sat up in his chair.

"Maybe you forgot something," I said. "You know that you are always forgetting things."

I could see him concentrate.

"Mom's birthday is in March," I said. "So that can't be it."

Mila couldn't contain herself. "Mr. Jones, did you forget your wedding anniversary?"

My fathers eyes lit up like a pinball machine. He slapped both hands against his face. "Oh, no," he cried. "No wonder she's been so mad at me. Ugh, I'm in big trouble, Jigsaw. This is double trouble. Twenty wonderful years of marriage and I forgot! Your mother will never forgive me!"

Mila coughed. "Pearl earrings are nice," she suggested.

My father's eyes widened. He smiled. "Pearl earrings!"

"Big ones," Mila advised.

"That's it," my father exclaimed. "I'll go to Klonsky's Jewelers in the morning. I'll take her out to dinner. I'll . . . I'll . . ."

"Beg forgiveness?" I offered.

My father stood up. "I'm such a fool," he said. And then he marched out of the room in search of my mother.

"It will be all right," Mila said. "Pearl earrings should do the trick."

I shrugged. I guessed so. I mean, I wouldn't know. But then again, I'm not from Venus.

# About the Author

James Preller often draws upon his own life as a basis for his Jigsaw Jones books. Like Jigsaw, James Preller has a slobbering, sock-eating dog. Like Jigsaw, James was the youngest in a large family. His older brothers called him Worm and worse — yeesh! And so do Jigsaw's!

James and Jigsaw both love jigsaw puzzles, baseball, grape juice, and mysteries! But even though Jigsaw and James have so much in common, they are not the same person.

Unlike Jigsaw, James Preller is the author of more than 80 books for children, including *The Big Book of Picture-Book Authors & Illustrators; Wake Me in Spring; Hiccups for Elephant;* and *Cardinal & Sunflower.* He lives outside of Albany, New York, with his wife, Lisa, three kids — Nicholas, Gavin, and Maggie — his cat, Blue, and his dog, Seamus.

Get your kicks from

# BLACK BELT

THE **BLACK BELT CLUB**

*Seven Wheels of Power*

by **DAWN BARNES**

ILLUSTRATED BY BERNARD CHANG

Join karate students Max, Maia, Antonio, and Jamie as they take on a terrible menace in their first secret martial-arts mission. Will these black belts find the strength and skill to battle danger and overcome evil? It will require courage, focus, and teamwork. But no matter what happens, these kids always try their best and never, ever give up!

Coming March

THE BLUE SKY PRESS

BBCT

# Take your imagination on a wild ride.

## THE SECRETS OF DROON

### Under the stairs, a magical world awaits you.

## Ghostville Elementary™

Welcome to Sleepy Hollow Elementary. Everyone says the basement is haunted, but no one's ever gone downstairs to prove it. Until now. This year, Jeff and Cassidy's classroom is moving to the basement. And you thought your school was scary!

## BLACK LAGOON ADVENTURES

All the kids are afraid to perform in the Black Lagoon talent show. But they have to, because mean Mrs. Green says so. Too bad if your only talent is squirting milk from your nose!

Available wherever you buy books.

## www.scholastic.com

LITTLE APPLE

SCHOLASTIC

LAT1

**Jigsaw and his partner, Mila, know that mysteries are like jigsaw puzzles—you've got to look at all the pieces to solve the case!**

| | | |
|---|---|---|
| ____0-590-69125-2 | #1: The Case of Hermie the Missing Hamster | $3.99 US |
| ____0-590-69126-0 | #2: The Case of the Christmas Snowman | $3.99 US |
| ____0-590-69127-9 | #3: The Case of the Secret Valentine | $3.99 US |
| ____0-590-69129-5 | #4: The Case of the Spooky Sleepover | $3.99 US |
| ____0-439-08083-5 | #5: The Case of the Stolen Baseball Cards | $3.99 US |
| ____0-439-08094-0 | #6: The Case of the Mummy Mystery | $3.99 US |
| ____0-439-11426-8 | #7: The Case of the Runaway Dog | $3.99 US |
| ____0-439-11427-6 | #8: The Case of the Great Sled Race | $3.99 US |
| ____0-439-11428-4 | #9: The Case of the Stinky Science Project | $3.99 US |
| ____0-439-11429-2 | #10: The Case of the Ghostwriter | $3.99 US |
| ____0-439-18473-8 | #11: The Case of the Marshmallow Monster | $3.99 US |
| ____0-439-18474-6 | #12: The Case of the Class Clown | $3.99 US |
| ____0-439-18476-2 | #13: The Case of the Detective in Disguise | $3.99 US |
| ____0-439-18477-0 | #14: The Case of the Bicycle Bandit | $3.99 US |
| ____0-439-30637-X | #15: The Case of the Haunted Scarecrow | $3.99 US |
| ____0-439-30638-8 | #16: The Case of the Sneaker Sneak | $3.99 US |
| ____0-439-30639-6 | #17: The Case of the Disappearing Dinosaur | $3.99 US |
| ____0-439-30640-X | #18: The Case of the Bear Scare | $3.99 US |
| ____0-439-42628-6 | #19: The Case of the Golden Key | $3.99 US |
| ____0-439-42630-8 | #20: The Case of the Race Against Time | $3.99 US |
| ____0-439-42631-6 | #21: The Case of the Rainy Day Mystery | $3.99 US |
| ____0-439-55995-2 | #22: The Case of the Best Pet Ever | $3.99 US |
| ____0-439-55996-0 | #23: The Case of the Perfect Prank | $3.99 US |
| ____0-439-55998-7 | #24: The Case of the Glow-in-the-Dark Ghost | $3.99 US |
| ____0-439-66165-X | #25: The Case of the Vanishing Painting | $3.99 US |
| **Super Specials** | | |
| ____0-439-30931-X | #1: The Case of the Buried Treasure | $3.99 US |
| ____0-439-42629-4 | #2: The Case of the Million-Dollar Mystery | $3.99 US |
| ____0-439-55997-9 | #3: The Case of the Missing Falcon | $3.99 US |

Available wherever you buy books, or use this order form.

**Scholastic Inc., P.O. Box 7502, Jefferson City, MO 65102**

Please send me the books I have checked above. I am enclosing $_____ (please add $2.00 to cover shipping and handling). Send check or money order—no cash or C.O.D.s please.

Name_____Age_____

Address_____

City _____ State/Zip_____

Please allow four to six weeks for delivery. Offer good in the U.S. only. Sorry, mail orders are not available to residents of Canada. Prices subject to change.

SCHOLASTIC and associated logos are trademarks and/or registered trademarks of Scholastic Inc.

JJBL0205